ISBN 0 86037 460 2

MUSLIM CHILDREN'S LIBRARY

HILMY THE HIPPO SERIES

HILMY THE HIPPO
Learns About Death

Author *Rae Norridge*
Illustrator *Leigh Norridge Marucchi*
Designer *Nasir Cadir*
Co-ordinator *Anwar Cara*

Published by
The Islamic Foundation
Markfield Conference Centre
Ratby Lane, Markfield
Leicester LE67 9SY
United Kingdom

T (01530) 244 944
F (01530) 244 946
E i.foundation@islamic-foundation.org.uk
      publications@islamic-foundation.com

Quran House, PO Box 30611, Nairobi, Kenya

PMB 3193, Kano, Nigeria

British Library Cataloguing in Publication Data

Norridge, Rae
   Hilmy the hippo learns about death
   1. Hilmy the Hippo (Fictitious character) - Pictorial works
   - Juvenile fiction 2. Death - Pictorial works - Juvenile
   fiction 3. Children's stories - Pictorial works
   I. Title II. Islamic Foundation (Great Britain)
   823.9'2 [J]

ISBN 0860374602

HILMY THE HIPPO

Rae Norridge

HIPPO

Learns About Death

Illustrated by *Leigh Norridge Marucchi*

THE ISLAMIC FOUNDATION

One fine morning Hilmy splashed about in the water. The sun was high in the clear blue sky and all around the birds were singing. Hilmy was very happy.

He left the water and climbed up onto the sandy bank of his waterhole. Lying close by on the warm sand, was Hilmy's best friend, the blue dragonfly.

"*As-Salamu 'Alaykum*, Blue Dragonfly," called Hilmy. "Isn't it a fine day today?"

But Hilmy's friend did not answer. Hilmy walked over to the dragonfly, whose wings were spread out glistening in the morning light.

3

Once again Hilmy said, "*As-Salamu 'Alaykum*, Blue Dragonfly." And once again the dragonfly did not answer.

Hilmy sniffed the dragonfly and gently nudged his friend with his nose. The blue dragonfly lay motionless.

"Why do you not answer me, Dragonfly?" asked Hilmy, his voice filled with concern. Still the little dragonfly did not reply.

The green frog that lived among the reeds and water lilies emerged from beneath a lily pad. He too began to call the blue dragonfly. The plover that was nesting close by, left her eggs and came rushing over. She had loved the kind little dragonfly and was deeply concerned.

Soon all the creatures that lived around the waterhole began to gather around. The water monitor came ambling over the warm sand, his tongue flicking in and out. The weaver birds, who were busily weaving their nests in the overhanging branches, stopped their work and flew down to where the little dragonfly lay.

But as much as his friends called, the little blue dragonfly did not lift a wing or move his head. Hilmy knew then that his best friend had died.

One by one all the creatures left the dragonfly and returned to their nests and homes. Everyone was filled with great sadness.

Hilmy too was very sad as he stood beside his little friend. He had never thought the blue dragonfly would die.

From a nearby bush Hilmy heard someone calling him,
"*As-Salamu 'Alaykum*, Hilmy. Why do you look so sad?"

Hilmy turned around and saw his friend the chameleon.
The chameleon, of course, was very slow on his feet,
therefore was not aware of what had happened.

"*Wa 'Alaykum as-Salam*, Chameleon," replied Hilmy sadly.

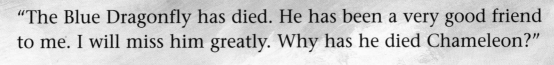

"The Blue Dragonfly has died. He has been a very good friend to me. I will miss him greatly. Why has he died Chameleon?"

The chameleon pondered for a short while. "I have no knowledge of these things, Hilmy. Perhaps you should go down to where the river runs through the forest. That is where the wise terrapin lives. He has lived for a long time. I know he will have the answers to all your questions."

"*Jazakallah Khair*, Chameleon," said Hilmy and with a heavy heart set out at once.

9

As he walked he thought a lot about his friend, the blue dragonfly, and all the friends he had ever known. He passed the mighty old lion, Claw. Since Hilmy was a large hippo, he had no need to fear Claw.

"*As-Salamu 'Alaykum*," Claw called Hilmy.
"*Wa 'Alaykum as-Salam*, Hilmy," answered Claw. "Where are you going? You look very sad."
"My best friend, the Blue Dragonfly, has died and I am going down to the forest to speak to the terrapin. He is very wise and perhaps he can tell me about life in the Hereafter."

"He is indeed very wise," replied Claw and lay down to sleep.
"You are very old Claw. Will you die soon?" asked Hilmy.

11

The old sleepy lion replied, "We all die at a time appointed for us by Allah, though we do not know the exact time of our death. But I am not afraid; I am ready when Allah calls me. I hope I have lived a good and just life. *Insha' Allah*, when I die, May Allah will have Mercy on me."

"*Fi Amanillah*," called Hilmy, with his heart filled with sorrow. "I must be on my way."

Soon Hilmy reached the forest. He made his way through the thick trees and dense undergrowth. In the distance Hilmy heard the river splashing and swirling over the rocks. He hurriedly followed the path. Once he was at the water's edge, Hilmy saw, in the clearing, the wise terrapin sunning himself on some rocks.

"*Assalamu Alaykum*, Terrapin," called Hilmy.
"*Wa 'Alaykum as-Salam*, Hilmy," replied the terrapin. "What has brought you all this way Hilmy? It is very far from your waterhole."

"My best friend, the blue dragonfly, has died and I am very sad," replied Hilmy. "I was told by the little chameleon you can answer some of my questions."

14

The sun streamed through the canopy of the trees, bathing the rocks with its warmth. The wise terrapin turned and faced Hilmy. "You must not grieve too much Hilmy. *Inna Lillahi wa inna ilayhi Raji'un*. We all belong to God and there comes a time when we must return to Him."

The forest was very beautiful; everything was lush and green. The river ran swiftly and was clear and bright. Hilmy knew this was all Allah's creation.

"What will happen to my friend now that he has died?" asked Hilmy, filled with concern.

"We hope the blue dragonfly will be given Allah's Mercy," replied the wise terrapin. "When we die we will have to face Allah and give an account of our life in this world. Those of us who have been good in this life will be given Paradise as a reward."

The wise Terrapin looked over the bright sparkling river as it gurgled over the rocks.

"We must ask Allah to forgive the blue dragonfly for any wrongs that he might have done," continued the terrapin. "So that God will admit him into Paradise."

Hilmy nodded his head deep in thought. He hoped the blue dragonfly had lived his life according to God's commands, but nevertheless he would pray to Allah to show Mercy on his little friend.

"If we are not good, and we do not live our lives according to
God's commands," asked Hilmy. "What will happen to us then?"

The wise old terrapin shook his head. "Then Hilmy," he said.
"We will be punished in Hell."

19

"On my journey here," said Hilmy, deep in thought. "I met Claw, the lion. He is very old now and soon he will die."

"Yes Hilmy," replied the terrapin. "But no one knows when we will die. Sometimes there are those of us who will die when we are young, and there will be some of us who will die when we are old. We do not know why. It is Allah's will."

20

Once again Hilmy nodded his head in deep thought. All the birds in the trees were quiet, as they too were listening to the wise terrapin. The happy cat-fish popped his head out of the water to hear what the terrapin was saying. The tree snake hung down from the branches, he too was listening with keen interest. A group of small butterflies flew down and settled on the flowers growing at the water's edge.

21

"We must live a decent life on this earth, Hilmy," continued the terrapin. "Whatever we think or do must be just and right. We must live a good and peaceful life if we are to be granted Paradise. God will judge us on the Day of Judgement and we cannot escape God's punishment. God will know how we have lived our lives. If we are bad, God will know. If we are good, God will know. Life in the Hereafter is infinite, that means it will never end, it is forever."

"*Jazakallah Khair*, Terrapin," said Hilmy as he turned to leave. "I have learned much today. *Fi Amanillah.*"

Hilmy had a lot to think about on his return to his waterhole. The sun dropped low on the horizon, turning the sky a brilliant gold. The waterhole shimmered in the golden light.

23

The little chameleon was there to greet him on his return, and all the birds chirped in greeting. Hilmy would miss the friendship he had with the blue dragonfly. But *Insha' Allah*, the blue dragonfly will be given Paradise for he had been a truly good friend, not only to Hilmy but to all the creatures who had shared their waterhole.

GLOSSARY
of Islamic Terms

As-Salamu 'Alaykum
Literally "Peace be upon you", the traditional Muslim greeting, offered when Muslims meet each other.

Wa 'Alaykum as-Salam
"Peace be upon you too", is the reply to the greeting, expressing their mutual love, sincerity and best wishes.

Insha' Allah
Literally "If Allah so wishes". Used by Muslims to indicate their decision to do something, provided they get help from Allah. It is recommended that whenever Muslims resolve to do something and make a promise, they should add "Insha' Allah".

Jazakallah Khair
Literally "May Allah give you a good reward". It is used for thanking someone who has done a favour to you and for any good act.

Fi Amanillah
Literally "In the safe custody of Allah". Used on the occasion of saying farewell to someone.

Inna Lillahi wa inna ilayhi Raji'un
"Undoubtedly we are for Allah and to Him is the return". It is used on hearing about someone's death or on suffering a loss. It reaffirms the Islamic belief that Allah is All-Powerful and that man is bound by His decrees.

Some information about
the Animals and Insects

Water Monitor
It is also known as the Nile monitor, which can grow as large as seven feet in length. Water monitors are strong swimmers and are found in all major rivers and lakes in Africa. They lay 20-60 eggs, which take nearly a year to hatch. They eat crabs, frogs, fish, bird and crocodile eggs, rodents and birds.

Weaver Birds
Weaver birds are so named because they weave basket shaped nests. The nests are built in reed beds or at the end of thin branches, which over-hang water. This prevents predators, such as snakes, from entering the nests to steal their eggs.

Chameleon
Chameleons are very slow moving. They live in trees and bushes and can change their colour to match their surroundings. Their eyes work independently, which means they can look in front as well as behind at the same time. A chameleon's tongue is longer than its body. All chameleons have poor hearing. Their diet consists of insects.

Terrapin
Terrapins are reptiles, which are found in rivers and lakes. They eat waterweeds, frogs, and sometimes catch birds drinking at the water's edge.

ORCHIDS

THE NEW PLANT LIBRARY

ORCHIDS

ANDREW MIKOLAJSKI

Consultant: Brian Rittershausen
Photography by Peter Anderson

LORENZ BOOKS

First published in 1999 by Lorenz Books

© Anness Publishing Limited 1999

Lorenz Books is an imprint of Anness Publishing Limited
Hermes House, 88–89 Blackfriars Road, London SE1 8HA

Published in the USA by Lorenz Books, Anness Publishing Inc.,
27 West 20th Street, New York, NY 10011; (800) 354 9657

This edition distributed in Canada by Raincoast Books,
8680 Cambie Street, Vancouver, British Columbia V6P 6M9

ISBN 0 7548 0125 X

A CIP catalogue record for this book is available from the British Library.

Publisher: Joanna Lorenz
Senior Editor: Caroline Davison
Designer: Ian Sandom
Production Controller: Karina Han

Printed and bound in Hong Kong/China

1 3 5 7 9 10 8 6 4 2

Acknowledgements: the publishers would like to thank Brian and Wilma
Rittershausen for allowing their orchids to be photographed at Burnham
Nurseries, in Devon, England, for the purposes of this book.

■ HALF TITLE PAGE
Laeliocattleya Lilac Dream ×
Casitas Spring
■ FRONTISPIECE
Dendrobium Mousmée
■ TITLE PAGE
Cattleya harrisoniana ×
Penny Karoda
■ RIGHT
Laeliocattleya Mini Purple
'Pinafore'

■ OPPOSITE TOP LEFT
Phragmipedium
Eric Young
■ OPPOSITE TOP RIGHT
Odontoglossum luteopurpureum
× Stonehurst Yellow
■ OPPOSITE BOTTOM LEFT
Sanderara Rippon Tor
'Burnham'
■ OPPOSITE BOTTOM RIGHT
Oncidium Sharry Baby

Contents

Introduction

*B*eautiful, flamboyant, sometimes bizarre: orchids exert a unique appeal. Everything about them is interesting, from their strange habit of growth, nestling on fallen tree trunks or among rocks or clambering skywards to the tree canopy, to their striking, often intoxicatingly scented flowers. Formerly considered plants for the connoisseur only, nowadays there is a huge range of hybrids that are easy to grow and affordable for all gardeners.

This book provides a complete introduction to this fascinating plant family, with information on their origins in the wild and their place in garden history, as well as advice on how best to display them. It also illustrates some of the most beautiful orchids now available and gives complete details on how to care for and propagate them.

■ RIGHT
Given proper care, orchids reward the gardener with an abundance of exotic-looking flowers.

Orchids in the wild

Orchids (Orchidaceae) comprise one of the largest families in the plant kingdom, numbering some 25,000 species in 835 genera, with over 100,000 hybrids. They represent almost 10 per cent of all flowering plants in the wild. The exact number of orchids cannot be calculated, because the orchid family constantly fluctuates in size. There are a number of reasons for this fluctuation: new species are still being discovered; different species and genera show a propensity to cross, resulting in a stream of new plants; and the destruction of much of their natural habitat means that species are, unfortunately, being lost in the wild.

Orchid habitats

Orchids are found in every continent except Antarctica, in environments that range from European meadowland to tropical rainforests. Those from the northern temperate zones are usually found in bogs, prairies, grassland and deciduous forests, and are predominantly terrestrial (in other words they root into the ground, like most other plants). The North American *Habenaria ciliaris* is so widespread as to be virtually a weed.

The majority of orchids, however, occur in the wet tropics, in a range of altitudes from sea level to at least 4,600m (15,000ft) above. They are predominantly epiphytic, i.e. growing on trees above the ground (from the Greek *epi*, upon, and *phyton*, plant), and derive their nutrients from small

■ LEFT
Maxillaria rufescens is an epiphytic orchid that is widespread in the tropical Americas.

■ BELOW
Phalaenopsis fasciata is a tropical species
native to the Philippines.

amounts of leaf litter and other
organic matter that collect in the
forks of the trees, and also from
minute traces of these foods dissolved
in atmospheric mists. A few are
lithophytic, growing in the cracks
between rocks (derived from the
Greek *lithos*, meaning stone).

Most are found in cloud forest,
generally on mountainsides, where
the cloud cover is virtually constant.
In such areas, which are also the
habitat of numerous mosses and
lichens, the slope of the ground
means that light can penetrate
through the trees to the vegetation on

the ground. This habitat also favours
members of the family Gesneriaceae
(which includes *Gloxinia*, *Saintpaulia*,
Sinningia and *Streptocarpus*), Araceae
(including *Calla* and *Monstera*), as
well as ferns and other epiphytic
plants. Orchids are not common on
flat ground in the rainforest. It is

useful to have an understanding of the typical habitat of orchids, because this provides clues to the cultivation of their exotic hybrids in the home.

A few species occur in the Arctic and there are even some that thrive in deserts: several epiphytic species occur in Peru in conjunction with cacti. There are also several lithophytic orchids native to Jamaica.

In evolutionary terms, orchids are among the youngest members of the plant kingdom and have evolved highly specialized ways of growing and breeding. Few are widespread, and most have adapted to specific local conditions, being dependent not only on local climate, but also on the presence of particular pollinators – usually insects, but sometimes bats and

birds. Some have flowers that mimic the females of some insect species, in order to attract the male, who then carries pollen to neighbouring plants.

Nearly all the orchids in the wild are under threat, owing to the destruction of their natural habitat, although nowadays the collecting of orchids in the wild is prohibited by law. Some species in cultivation are

■ RIGHT

Vanilla polylepis, from Kenya to Zimbabwe, produces large seed pods that are dried for use as a food flavouring.

known to be already extinct in the wild, but a recent trend by nature conservationists is to grow them under controlled conditions and then reintroduce them to the wild. In many cases, this became possible only once the germination requirements of individual species were understood.

Commercial value

Few orchids have commercial value, apart from *Vanilla planifolia,* which is grown for the production of vanilla, a valuable ingredient of foods and perfumes. *V. pompona, V. polylepis* and *V. tahitensis* are also grown for the same purpose. *V. planifolia* is native to Mexico, but today the main producer is Madagascar. Vanilla is also grown in French Polynesia, Réunion, Dominica, Indonesia, the West Indies, the Seychelles and Puerto Rico. Other orchids have been used medicinally in folk medicine. The tubers of some orchids are also ground down to make a substitute for flour.

■ LEFT

Some orchids, such as the terrestrial *Paphiopedilum gratrixianum* from Laos, have evolved specialized "pouches" in order to trap pollinating insects.

Orchid history

The Greek philosopher Theophrastus referred to orchids in his *Enquiry into Plants* around 370–285 BC. The plant he knew was the terrestrial *Orchis*, so named because of the similarity between its tuberous roots and testicles (*orkhis* in Greek means testicle). These roots, if crushed and eaten, were thought to increase sexual potency. Orchids are also known to have been cultivated in ancient China and Japan. They were grown for their beauty as well as their supposed aphrodisiac properties, and by 1700 enjoyed considerable status as connoisseurs' plants.

The North American terrestrial *Cypripedium acaule* was described by Parkinson in 1640 in his *Theatricum botanicum*. The first tropical orchid introduced into Europe was probably *Brassavola nodosa* (found in Mexico, Panama and Venezuela), then known as *Epidendrum nodosum*, which was grown in the Netherlands in the late 17th century. *Bletia purpurea*, from the Bahamas, was introduced into Great Britain in 1731.

At first, all epiphytic orchids were classified as *Epidendrum* (meaning "tree-dwelling"). It was soon realized, however, that a single genus could not encompass the wide variety of plants being discovered, so new genera were (and still are being) created.

Further imports were made during the 18th century, and by 1789 the collection of exotics at the Royal Botanic Gardens at Kew, in England, numbered 15. The Liverpool Botanic Garden also acquired an important early collection, and received the first *Cattleya* from Brazil in 1810.

The early decades of the 19th century saw the beginning of "orchidomania", a passion for orchids similar to the Tulipomania of the 17th century. It began almost by accident. Consignments of tropical plants crossed the Atlantic to Europe wrapped in the stems and foliage of other plants. William Cattley, of Barnet, north London, was intrigued by the "packaging" and succeeded in growing some of the plants. In 1818, one such plant produced a sensational

■ RIGHT
Phragmipedium besseae is a species from Peru discovered as recently as 1981. Its red colouring has made it valuable in hybridizing.

■ RIGHT
Cattleya warscewiczii is a beautiful species named in honour of the Lithuanian plant hunter Joseph Warscewicz, who discovered it. Its fragrant, pinkish mauve flowers appear from summer to autumn.

flower and was named in honour of Cattley as *Cattleya labiata*. The exact source of the original plant was discovered in 1836 on a mountain near Rio de Janeiro, where the trees that provided its habitat were being burnt for charcoal. Plant hunters were sent to look for more cattleyas. Their voracious collecting, together with the destruction of the forest for charcoal, led to a serious depletion of their numbers in the wild.

Plant hunting became a serious and even deadly pursuit, involving expeditions into uncharted and inhospitable jungles. The Lithuanian Joseph Warscewicz made several expeditions into Central and South America between 1840 and 1850 and is honoured by two species: *Cattleya warscewiczii* and *Miltonia warscewiczii*.

Commercial nurserymen ruthlessly exploited both the orchids' natural habitat and the hunters they sent to collect them. The high costs of employing plant hunters meant that the price of imported plants was extremely high: up to several hundred

pounds per plant. Unscrupulous collectors felled many trees to gain access to the orchids that grew in the upper canopy. Up to 10,000 specimens of a single species might be taken. As a result, many species are seen today only in botanic gardens.

The first recorded epiphytes to reach North America were sent to a John Booth of Massachusetts from his brother James who lived in London. In 1865, Edward Rand gave a large collection to Harvard University, and this has become the core of one of the world's most extensive orchid collections, housed at the Cambridge Botanic Gardens.

The first orchids in cultivation were tropical species that needed hot-house conditions. Once cooler-growing orchids, notably *Odontoglossum crispum* from South

America, were discovered and safely imported, however, orchids became accessible to a much wider public.

The first manmade hybrids appeared in 1853, when John Dominy of the Veitch nursery crossed two *Calanthe* species; the resulting hybrid first flowered in 1856. Germination proved troublesome, however, because the relationship between the seed and mycorrhizal fungi was not fully understood. It was later demonstrated that seeds could be germinated in test tubes on an agar solution into which the fungus had been introduced. In 1922, Dr Lewis Knudson of Cornell University created a formula of various chemicals combined with cane sugar, agar and water that made the presence of the fungus unnecessary. This opened the door on a new range of spectacular hybrids.

Starting an orchid collection

Before starting an orchid collection, it is a good idea to visit a specialist nursery, one of the larger flower shows or an orchid show. Details are usually announced in the gardening press or in specialized magazines. Most specialist nurseries also organize demonstrations and talks that provide valuable sources of information. Advice on all aspects of growing and caring for orchids will be freely given.

It is not necessary to build a dedicated orchid house in order to enjoy orchids at home. Modern breeding and propagation techniques have resulted in a range of hybrids that are both easy to grow and much less expensive than previously. Many make suitable houseplants and will thrive in the home, needing no special equipment or additional source of heating. Many will tolerate central heating, which other plants dislike. Others are ideal subjects for a conservatory or heated greenhouse, where it is easier to simulate tropical conditions. Orchids can be brought into a sitting room when in flower, then returned to their permanent quarters, without suffering harm.

Hybrid orchids can be divided into various groups, depending on their parentage. A large group is the cattleyas and laelias, which comprise not only the two genera themselves but also hybrids between these and other related genera. The group includes *Laeliocattleya*, *Brassolaeliocattleya* (involving *Brassia*) and *Sophrolaeliocattleya* (involving *Sophronitis*). They are sometimes all loosely referred to as "cattleyas". For many, these are the archetypal orchids, with their large, flamboyant flowers, often with frilled lips and

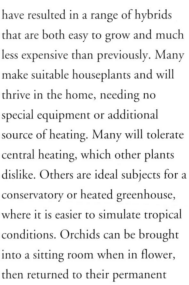

■ ABOVE
For many growers, cattleyas are the archetypal orchid, with their glamorous flowers. The plant illustrated here is the complex hybrid *Laeliocattleya* Lilac Dream × Casitas Spring.

■ LEFT
Cymbidium Summer Pearl is an easily grown hybrid that produces an abundance of creamy white flowers between autumn and spring.

■ BELOW
Anyone who becomes fascinated by orchids
will soon find their collection expanding.

petals, that appear in autumn and spring and last for about three weeks. The colours include rich, glowing mauves and purples, red, and soft pastel pinks. The flowers can also be marked with other colours, including white and yellow. Modern interbreeding has introduced green and blue into the range. Many are highly perfumed. Cattleyas make excellent cut flowers and were popular in corsages in the 1960s. They have retained their status as a florist's flower, though nowadays other orchids are equally worthy of attention. Being intermediate-growing, these robust plants are suitable for growing in a heated greenhouse or conservatory.

Miltoniopsis is the so-called "pansy" orchid, since their large, flat faces, which can be as much as 10cm (4in) across, resemble pansies. Some are also scented. They are available in a range of colours, the rich reds being deservedly popular. Most flower in summer, but they can also flower at other times.

Odontoglossum is related to *Miltoniopsis*. As with cattleyas, a huge range of hybrids has been produced, including *Odontioda* (with *Cochlioda*), *Odontocidium* (with *Oncidium*), *Vuylstekeara* (*Cochlioda*,

Miltonia and *Odontoglossum*) and *Wilsonara* (*Cochlioda*, *Odontoglossum* and *Oncidium*). They have colourful, showy flowers in a range of sizes. They do not have a specific flowering season, but flower when the current season's pseudobulb is mature; the flowers last for six to eight weeks.

Odontoglossums make fairly compact plants but are among the most striking of orchids, some producing hundreds of flowers on a single flower spike that can be up to 90cm (3ft) high. The flowers can persist on the plant for up to three months. Some odontoglossums can complete their annual growth cycle in

nine months, meaning that they will flower twice within 18 months, at opposite ends of the season. By judicious choice among the available hybrids, it is possible to have odonto-glossums in flower all year. This makes them a valued florist's flower.

Some *Odontoglossum* species come from Mexico and Guatemala, where the air is drier than in many typical orchid habitats. This tolerance of a dry atmosphere has been inherited by many of the hybrids, making it possible to grow them in centrally heated homes without too much difficulty, and thus widening the appeal of the orchid.

■ LEFT
A fine collection of *Phalaenopsis* hybrids in a large, heated conservatory.

Paphiopedilums are the well-known "slipper" orchids, easily identifiable by the lip, which is enlarged into an inflated pouch designed to trap pollinating insects. These are robust plants that tolerate low light levels, so are ideal for growing as houseplants. They usually flower throughout the winter, their flowers lasting for up to ten weeks or more, and are grown commercially to provide cut flowers. Of rather more subtle appeal than those of other orchids, these are often in shades of green, brown, copper and bronze, with stripes, veins and spots of different colours. Recent breeding has introduced white and soft pink into the range. Some have the added

distinction of mottled leaves. Green-leaved varieties are for the most part cool-growing and thrive in a cool greenhouse. Those with mottled leaves generally require higher temperatures and do well in an indoor growing case, so if you are planning a collection of these plants, check that they all have the same temperature requirements. Those with marbled leaves, from South-east Asia, are smaller and have pale flowers in white, yellow and pink. They

combine well with phalaenopsis, but require slightly drier conditions. Paphiopedilums are best allowed to form large clumps and should be divided less often than other orchids.

Phragmipediums are similar to paphiopedilums but the plants are less often grown, owing to the difficulty of finding plants in the wild. The lateral petals are considerably extended and are also twisted. There are relatively few hybrids.

Phalaenopsis are sometimes referred to as "moth" orchids, because the flowers look like resting moths. They are among the most popular orchids, being warm-growing and thus well adapted to the high temperatures of most modern sitting rooms, besides producing their attractive flowers virtually year round. The flower stem continues to grow after it has flowered in order to produce further flower buds, thus

■ RIGHT
Small orchids can be effectively displayed in glass cases or, as here, in an old fish tank.

■ RIGHT
Gongora truncata, from South America, is best grown in a hanging basket so that its flowers hang at eye level.

■ BELOW
The flowers of this *Cymbidium* Summer Pearl 'Sonia' are produced between late summer and spring.

ensuring a flowering display that can last for several months.

Phalaenopsis have thick, fleshy leaves. On some plants, these are plain green, whilst others have leaves that are mottled and barred with lighter green and silvery grey. Related genera include *Vanda*, *Renanthera* and *Doritis*. They are widely distributed in the wild, but most grown today originate from the Philippines. They thrive in a growing case and can also look attractive when grown in a hanging basket or on a cork "raft" suspended from the ceiling, with the leaves facing downwards.

Cymbidiums are deservedly popular and are among the easiest to grow. They can flower from autumn through to the following late spring, the flower spikes lasting up to six to eight weeks or more. They make large plants, however, so need a lot of room. They are cool-growing, so if you are planning to use them in the home, they should be moved in winter to a cool, light room, such as an unheated bedroom, since they are not especially tolerant of central heating. In summer, they can be placed out of doors, but in a position out of direct sunlight at the hottest part of the day. This will also ensure a

good drop in temperature overnight, which is needed for successful flowerbud formation. Although there are many species in the wild, found in China, Japan, Korea and north Australia, only a few species are in general cultivation, and these have largely been superseded by the many hybrids that have been produced.

Displaying orchids

Many orchids are suitable for growing on windowsills. Grouping orchids together creates a favourable microclimate, since it encourages humidity. If you want to grow certain orchids that are not adapted to the prevailing conditions, you could consider growing them in a case. Very sophisticated models that are like mini-greenhouses, suitable for warm- and intermediate-growing orchids, have heating cables, lighting and

ventilators to provide the plants with the optimum growing conditions. At less expense, you can improvise a case out of a fish tank, left open at the top. The temperature and humidity will be a few points higher inside the case than out, but you will obviously have less control over exact levels.

Orchids with trailing stems are best in hanging baskets or in pots on high shelves so that the flowers are at eye level. Good companion plants that tolerate the same conditions as most orchids include *Begonia rex*, *Spathiphyllum*, *Monstera*, the very tolerant *Ficus benjamina*, bromeliads, rainforest cacti such as *Rhipsalis* and *Schlumbergera*, and a wide variety of tender ferns.

Orchid botany and nomenclature

Orchids are primarily herbaceous or evergreen perennials. They range in size from *Dendrophylax*, a plant that is reduced simply to roots, to the huge, bamboo-like *Arundina*. Orchids are distinguished from other plant families by the distinctive structure of their flowers.

How orchids grow

Terrestrial orchids, native mainly to temperate regions, are rooted in the ground like most other plants, and have either a rhizome (a swollen horizontal stem) or an underground tuber (a structure with a similar function but without the tendency to grow laterally). From these arise rosettes of leaves from which flower stems appear. Most experience a period of dormancy. For herbaceous species with rhizomes, this usually occurs in winter, whilst tuberous species are dormant in summer. Evergreens rest either in winter or just after flowering.

Epiphytic orchids, most of which are evergreen, spend their lives above ground and have special aerial roots that allow them to cling to trees or rocks (in which case they are more correctly referred to as lithophytic). The roots can absorb nutrients and minerals from moisture in the air, rainwater, bird droppings that wash down the tree, and decayed plant matter that collects around them. They do not derive nourishment from the host tree directly, so are not parasites. Most experience a period of dormancy, usually in the dry season, when growth slows down or even stops altogether. Tropical species from near the Equator, however, will grow and flower virtually continuously.

Epiphytes have two main habits of growth. In sympodial growth, as can be observed in cattleyas and odonto-glossums, the stems spread horizontally and become rootlike. Such stems can be referred to as

■ ABOVE
Sympodial orchids, such as the cymbidium shown here, have swollen stems called pseudobulbs. Older bulbs (backbulbs) lose their leaves as the plant grows ever outwards, but remain live.

■ LEFT
Stenoglottis fimbriata is a terrestrial orchid from South Africa.

■ RIGHT
Vandas are
monopodial
orchids whose
stems grow ever
upwards.

rhizomes. From these arise swollen
vertical organs that store food and
water. These thickened stems look
like bulbs (hence their name of
"pseudobulbs") and nourish the
plant while it is dormant. Most
pseudobulbs are oval and can be up
to 10cm (4in) long. Sympodial
orchids produce at least one new
pseudobulb each season. The bulbs
outlive the foliage, which dies back
after three or four years, and persist as
dormant bulbs (or "backbulbs") that
support the younger, flower- and leaf-
bearing pseudobulbs. Backbulbs can
be used for propagation. Flower
spikes emerge from the base of the
leading bulb or from the apex of the
bulb. Sympodial orchids mainly
occur in rainforests at sea level or
low altitudes.

By contrast, orchids with a
monopodial habit produce stems that
grow upwards, to all intents and
purposes indefinitely. Roots can be
produced on the upper portions of
the stem. In the wild, monopodial

orchids such as *Vanilla* and *Vanda*
clamber upwards through dense
jungle towards the tree canopy. They
produce branched, sometimes arching
flower stems that arise from inside
one or other of the basal leaves.
Monopodial epiphytes are usually
native to dense, misty rainforests at
higher altitudes.

A few orchids exhibit a third
manner of growth, defined as
diapodial. Their habit is similar to
sympodial orchids, but on these
plants no pseudobulbs are formed.

Orchid flowers

Orchid flowers are composed of six
segments, collectively referred to as
the perianth: these comprise three
sepals, which enclose the unopened
flower, and three petals inside. In
most plants, the sepals are green and
are hidden by the open flower. In the
case of orchids, however, they are
usually petal-like and are marked and
coloured in a similar fashion to the

true petals. The lowest of the three
petals, called the lip or labellum, is
modified in shape and serves as a
landing platform for pollinating
insects. This structure represents a
peak in plant adaptation to specific
pollinators, and the petals may guide
insects to the lip with their colouring.
In some orchids, the lip is inflated
and forms a pouch or "slipper", as in
the case of *Paphiopedilum*.

Orchid flowers are distinct
(though not unique) in that they are
symmetrical only from side to side
and not from top to bottom. They
are produced singly, in a spray (or
raceme) or on a branched spike.

■ ABOVE
This phragmipedium has striped petals
that guide pollinating insects towards its
inflated pouch.

■ LEFT
Polystachya species produce racemes of tiny flowers.

Orchids flower at different seasons of the year. Some, however, can flower at any time of year, whilst others will flower on and off throughout the year. The flower spikes are mostly long-lasting, but in a few species the flowers last for only a day. Flower size also varies, from those no more than 2mm (0.1in) across (*Pleurothallis*) to those measuring 38cm (15in) from one sepal tip to the other (*Brassia*).

The wide diversity of flower structures reflects the fact that each has developed individual pollination methods. In the wild, pollinators include spiders and hummingbirds, as well as insects. White flowers with a strong scent have evolved to attract nocturnal insects, usually moths; their scent is typically sweet or musky. Butterflies are more likely to be attracted to brightly coloured flowers, and these too can be fragrant. Bird-pollinated orchids are also usually brightly coloured, predominantly in reds, blues and yellows. They tend to lack scent, since birds have little sense of smell, if any. Some orchids attract flies by a means of deception, having the smell of rotting meat or animal dung. Flower colours of these are usually dull green, brown, purple or red. Some orchids (e.g. *Bulbophyllum* and *Masdevallia*) have long, tail-like petals that wave in the air and act as an attractant to flies. Others have fringed petals that fulfil the same purpose. Some species mimic the odours of female insects in order to attract pollinating males.

Orchid seed

Orchid seed is dustlike and is dispersed by the wind, often over great distances. The seed consists of a dry outer coat surrounding a mass of undifferentiated cells that form a pre-embryo. There is no endosperm to nourish the embryo. Nutrition is generally supplied by a fungus called a mycorrhyzum, which both attacks the embryo and supports it. The fungus later helps the plant to take up nutrients and also prevents nutrients from leaching out of the roots. Each is dependent on the other for its own

Oncidium

Cymbidium

Dendrobium

survival. (This phenomenon is not unique to orchids: a number of forest trees and heathers have a similar relationship with root fungi.)

Nomenclature

Botanists use the binomial system to name plant species: the genus name (e.g. *Vanda*) followed by the species name (e.g. *caerulea*). These names are always printed in italic type when naming a plant. All the species in a genus are genetically distinct from each other, but share some characteristics. A cultivar (the name given to a "cultivated variety") is different in appearance from the species but is nevertheless genetically identical to it. Cultivar names are printed in roman type between single quotation marks (e.g. 'Alba').

In the plant kingdom generally, hybridization between some species is possible and can occur in nature. In the specific case of orchids, some genera will also cross with each other to produce intergeneric hybrids such as *Laeliocattleya*, which is a cross between *Laelia* and *Cattleya*. Crosses involving three or more genera can also be made.

Multiple crosses produce groups of hybrids known as grexes. The progeny of any cross will be genetically unique but will share certain characteristics with the parents. Grex names are printed in roman type without single quotation marks, whilst names of individual selections within the group are placed in single quotation marks. Hence, for example, in the case of *Brassolaeliocattleya* Hetherington Horace 'Coronation', "Hetherington Horace" is the name of the grex. Most cultivated orchids are complex hybrids of this kind. Present conventions governing the naming of orchid hybrids dictate that all the offspring of any two parents must bear the same grex name.

Orchids have the most systematically compiled stud book of any family of plants: the *International Register of Orchid Hybrids*. You need not be put off by the convoluted names. The names merely reflect the fact that hybridizers have, over the years, kept meticulous records of their crosses so that the parentage of nearly all orchids in cultivation can be determined. This is not the case with such heavily interbred garden plants as roses and rhododendrons, for instance, for which detailed knowledge is lacking and has to be assumed.

Understanding any orchid's parentage from the information in the *International Register* can provide significant and helpful clues as to its correct care and cultivation.

Beallara

Phalaenopsis

Miltoniopsis

Unless otherwise stated, all the orchids described here are evergreen. They are classified as cool-, intermediate- or warm-growing (for further details, see 'How to grow orchids'). For hints on cultivation of the individual genera and the parentage of intergeneric hybrids, refer to the 'Orchid checklist'.

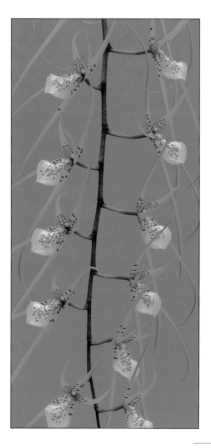

■ ABOVE
ASPASIA LUNATA 'A'

Epiphytic orchid, a selection of a species from Brazil. In summer, it has starlike flowers, banded and spotted green and brown, with pinkish white lips. The pseudobulbs are roughly oval. Intermediate-growing.

■ LEFT
BRASSIA VERRUCOSA 'SEA MIST'

Epiphytic orchid, a selection of a species from south Mexico to Venezuela. In summer, arching stems, up to 75cm (30in) long, carry spiderlike, musk-scented, greenish yellow flowers. The pseudobulbs are roughly oval to oblong. Cool-growing. *Brassia verrucosa* 'Sea Mist' is suitable for a growing case.

■ ABOVE

BRASSOLAELIOCATTLEYA ENID MOORE ×
LAELIOCATTLEYA STARTING POINT

Epiphytic orchid. In late summer to autumn, it produces large,
showy, creamy white flowers with ruffled petal edges; the lips are
heavily stained with rich rosy purple and have yellow centres lined
with purple. The pseudobulbs are erect and club-shaped. Cool- to
intermediate-growing.

■ RIGHT

BULBOPHYLLUM LOBBII

Epiphytic orchid from north-east India, south-east Asia and the
Philippines. In early summer, solitary pale yellow, red and yellow
or ochre flowers are produced that are veined red or speckled pink
and yellow, and lined brown. The pseudobulbs are roughly oval.
Bulbophyllum lobbii has a creeping habit. Intermediate-growing.

■ ABOVE

BURRAGEARA LIVING FIRE 'REDMAN'
(*VUYLSTEKEARA* EDNA × *ONCIDIUM*
MACULATUM)

Epiphytic orchid. Mature plants produce spikes of bright red
flowers throughout the year. Cool-growing.

■ ABOVE

CATTLEYA ENID × *BRASSOLAELIOCATTLEYA*
HOLIDAY INN

Epiphytic orchid. In late summer to autumn, it produces huge
white flowers with ruffled petal edges; the lips are stained with rich
rosy purple and have pale greenish yellow centres. The pseudobulbs
are erect and club-shaped. Cool- to intermediate-growing.

■ LEFT

CATTLEYA HARRISONIANA ×
PENNY KARODA

Epiphytic orchid. In summer and
autumn, it produces solitary, rich pink
flowers with ruffled petal edges; the
trumpet-shaped lips are light violet-pink
shading to rich purplish pink at the edges
and with yellow centres. The pseudobulbs
are erect and club-shaped. Cool- to
intermediate-growing.

■ LEFT

CATTLEYA LODDIGESII 'ALBA' × OLD WHITEY

Epiphytic orchid. From late summer to autumn, it produces large, solitary, luminous violet flowers with ruffled petal edges. The lips are elongated, are marked with rosy purple and have yellow centres. The pseudobulbs are erect and club-shaped. Cool- to intermediate-growing.

■ RIGHT

CATTLEYA LOUIS CARLA × *BRASSOLAELIOCATTLEYA* NICKIE HOLGUIN

Epiphytic orchid. In late summer and autumn it bears large, showy, creamy white flowers that have ruffled petal edges and lips stained yellow in the centre. The pseudobulbs are erect and club-shaped. Cool- to intermediate-growing.

■ FAR RIGHT

COELOGYNE MASSANGEANA

Epiphytic orchid from Malaysia, Sumatra and Java. In early spring to summer, hanging stems carry up to 20 scented, pale yellow flowers with brown and yellow lips. The pseudobulbs are cone-shaped. Intermediate-growing. *Coelogyne massangeana* should be kept dry in winter; it is effective on an orchid raft.

■ LEFT

COELOGYNE MEM. W. MICHOLITZ

Epiphytic orchid. From spring to summer, it produces spikes of creamy white flowers; the lips are spotted with red and yellow. The pseudobulbs are cylindrical to rounded. Cool-growing.

■ RIGHT

CYMBIDIUM MAUREEN GRAPES 'MARILYN'

Epiphytic orchid. From autumn to spring, it produces erect spikes of greenish yellow flowers; the lips are spotted red towards the edge. The pseudobulbs are rounded. Cool-growing.

■ RIGHT

CYMBIDIUM SUMMER PEARL 'SENNA'

Epiphytic orchid. Between autumn and spring, it produces erect spikes of greenish yellow flowers; the lips are heavily spotted with maroon. The pseudobulbs are rounded. Cool-growing.

■ BELOW

CYMBIDIUM SUMMER PEARL 'SONIA'

Epiphytic orchid. Between late summer and spring, it produces erect spikes of creamy pink flowers; the lips are heavily spotted with maroon. The pseudobulbs are rounded. Cool-growing.

■ LEFT

DENDROBIUM EMMA GOLD

Epiphytic orchid. From summer to autumn, tall, upright stems carry small, greenish yellow flowers with maroon lips. The pseudobulbs are elongated and stemlike. Cool-growing.

■ RIGHT

DENDROBIUM MOUSMÉE

Epiphytic orchid. In summer, pendent trusses of
mauve-tinged, white flowers with rich yellow lips
hang from the tops of strong, upright canes. The
pseudobulbs are narrow and stemlike. Cool-growing.
An old cultivar, *Dendrobium* Mousmée is similar in
appearance to the species *D. thyrsiflorum*.

■ BELOW

ENCYCLIA COCHLEATA

Epiphytic orchid found from Florida to Mexico,
Colombia and Venezuela. Its ribbonlike flowers, which
are pale green with deep purple lips, can be produced
at any time of year. Pseudobulbs are flattened pear-
shaped. Cool-growing.

■ LEFT

ENCYCLIA FRAGRANS

Epiphytic orchid from south
Mexico, Central America, the
Greater Antilles and Brazil.
In spring and summer, it has
racemes of scented, cream to
greenish white flowers with
maroon-striped lips. The
pseudobulbs are narrowly
ovoid to ellipsoid. Cool-
growing.

ENCYCLIA VITELLINA 'BURNHAM STAR'

Epiphytic orchid, a selection of a species from Mexico and Guatemala. From spring to summer, it produces panicles of orange-red to scarlet flowers with orange to yellow lips. The pseudobulbs are roughly oval to conical. Cool-growing.

EPIDENDRUM PINK CASCADE

Epiphytic orchid. In summer, tall, arching stems carry hanging clusters of small, white-tinged, mauve flowers. Cool- to intermediate-growing.

EPIDENDRUM PLASTIC DOLL

Epiphytic orchid. In summer, it produces hanging clusters of small, pale green flowers, sometimes marked pink in the centre, with yellow lips. Cool- to intermediate-growing. *Epidendrum* Plastic Doll will flower as a small plant.

■ LEFT
GONGORA MACULATA

Epiphytic orchid from Mexico, Central
America, northern South America and
Trinidad. In summer, it produces hanging
racemes of small, thin-textured flowers
that are pale yellow with red spotting and
banding, or red-brown with pale yellow
spotting. The pseudobulbs are roughly oval
to pear-shaped. Intermediate-growing.

■ ABOVE

LAELIA PULCHERRIMA 'ALBA'

Epiphytic orchid. In summer, it produces
large, pure white, fragrant flowers. The
pseudobulbs are slender. Cool-growing.

■ RIGHT

LAELIOCATTLEYA
CANYONLANDS ×
SOPHROLAELIOCATTLEYA
JEWELER'S ART

Epiphytic orchid. In summer and into
autumn, it produces spectacular,
luminous mauve flowers; the lips are deep
purple, with ruffled edges and yellow-
orange markings. The pseudobulbs are
erect and club-shaped. Cool- to
intermediate-growing.

■ RIGHT

LAELIOCATTLEYA LOVE
FANTASY 'SWEET DREAMS'
Epiphytic orchid. From late summer to
autumn, it produces racemes of large,
showy, white flowers with lips that are
splashed rosy purple and have yellow
centres. The pseudobulbs are cylindrical.
Cool-growing.

■ BELOW

LAELIOCATTLEYA MINI
PURPLE 'PINAFORE'

Epiphytic orchid. From late summer to
autumn, it produces large, rosy purple
flowers with trumpet-like lips that are
stained darker at the tips and have yellow
centres. The pseudobulbs are cylindrical.
Cool-growing.

■ LEFT

LAELIOCATTLEYA
TINY TREASURE ×
LAKE CASITAS

Epiphytic orchid. In summer
and autumn, it produces
spectacular white flowers, with
ruffled petal edges and lips that
are stained reddish purple at
the edge and yellow towards the
centre. Cool-growing.

■ LEFT

LYCASTE DEPPEI

Deciduous epiphytic orchid from Mexico and Guatemala. In spring to summer, it produces masses of flowers, up to 11.5cm (4½in) across, with green sepals spotted with reddish brown, white petals flecked with brown and deep yellow lips marked red. The pseudobulbs are oval. Cool-growing. Keep the foliage dry in summer.

■ ABOVE

MASDEVALLIA WHISKERS

Epiphytic orchid. In summer, it produces solitary flowers that have yellow-orange, long-tailed sepals, heavily spotted with red, surrounding insignificant petals and lips. It lacks pseudobulbs. Cool-growing. Do not allow to dry out in winter.

■ RIGHT

MILTONIA CLOWESII

Epiphytic orchid from Brazil. In autumn, stems up to 60cm (2ft) long each carry six to ten starlike, yellowish green flowers, tinged with maroon and heavily blotched and barred brown. The lips are white, with a pinkish mauve blotch on the upper part. The pseudobulbs are narrowly ovoid. Cool-growing. Misting in summer can mark the foliage, so provide humidity by other means. It is suitable for growing on a windowsill.

■ LEFT

MILTONIA WARSCEWICZII 'ALBA'

Epiphytic orchid, a selection of a species from Peru, Colombia and Costa Rica. In summer, it produces fragrant, yellow and white flowers. The oblong to roughly oval pseudobulbs are compressed sideways. Intermediate-growing.

■ RIGHT

MILTONIOPSIS FALDOUET

Epiphytic orchid. In summer, and occasionally at other times, it produces large, flat flowers that have velvety, deep red-maroon petals; the white lips are edged mauve and are streaked and spotted with maroon. The pseudobulbs are fleshy and roughly oval. Cool-growing.

■ LEFT

MILTONIOPSIS STORM

Epiphytic orchid. In summer, and occasionally at other times, it produces large, flat, pansy-like, rich red flowers that are marked with yellow and pink at the base of the lips. The pseudobulbs are fleshy and roughly oval. Cool-growing.

■ RIGHT

MILTONIOPSIS ST MARY

Epiphytic orchid. In summer, and occasionally at other times, it produces large, flat, white flowers; the lips have yellow centres that are marked with red. The pseudobulbs are fleshy and roughly oval. Cool-growing.

■ ABOVE

ODONTIODA MONT FELARD ×
ST AUBIN'S BAY

Neat-growing, epiphytic orchid. At varying
seasons, it produces spikes of white flowers
spotted with rich pink; the lips are stained
the same colour towards the edge and have
yellow centres. The petal edges are ruffled
and frilled. Cool-growing.

■ RIGHT

ODONTOCIDIUM TIGER
HAMBÜHREN 'BUTTERFLY'

Epiphytic orchid. In autumn, and also at
other times, it produces rich yellow flowers
mottled with chestnut brown. The
pseudobulbs are rounded. Cool-growing.

■ ABOVE

ODONTOGLOSSUM
GEYSER GOLD

Epiphytic orchid. Upright stems carry
showy flowers, yellow overlaid with darker
gold markings, at any time of year. The
pseudobulbs are roughly oval to conical.
Cool-growing.

■ LEFT

ONCIDIUM SHARRY BABY

Epiphytic orchid. From summer to
autumn, it produces tall, branching
stems that carry an abundance of small,
chocolate-scented flowers marked maroon
and white. Cool-growing.

■ BELOW LEFT

ODONTOGLOSSUM
LUTEOPURPUREUM ×
STONEHURST YELLOW

Epiphytic orchid. At varying times of the
year, depending on when the pseudobulb
is mature, it produces upright racemes of
bright yellow flowers that are barred and
blotched with dark red. The pseudobulbs
are roughly oval to conical. Cool-growing.

■ BELOW

PAPHIOPEDILUM ALFRED
HOLLINGTON

Terrestrial orchid. In autumn and winter,
it produces greenish brown flowers, heavily
spotted and striped with darker brown and
with deep "pouches". Cool- to
intermediate-growing.

■ RIGHT

PAPHIOPEDILUM AVALON
MIST

Terrestrial orchid. From spring to summer,
it produces yellowish green flowers; the
narrow petals have twisted edges,
and are spotted and lined with maroon.
There are no pseudobulbs. Cool- to
intermediate-growing.

■ FAR RIGHT

PAPHIOPEDILUM
CALLOSO-ARGUS

Terrestrial orchid. From spring to
summer, it produces solitary, green
flowers; the upper sepal is heavily striped
with maroon and the petals are spotted
with the same colour. The leaves are
mottled dark green. There are no
pseudobulbs. Cool- to intermediate-
growing.

■ RIGHT

PHALAENOPSIS EQUESTRIS

Epiphytic orchid from the Philippines and
Taiwan. From spring to winter, upright
stems carry small, soft pink flowers with
darker lips that are streaked with red.
There are no pseudobulbs. Warm-growing.

■ LEFT

PHALAENOPSIS LADY
SAKHARA

Epiphytic orchid. Throughout the year, it produces racemes of pink flowers that are veined darker; the lips are glowing cerise pink and have yellow centres. There are no pseudobulbs. Warm-growing.

■ BELOW

PHALAENOPSIS MYSTIC
GOLDEN LEOPARD

Epiphytic orchid. Throughout the year, it produces racemes of soft yellow flowers that are spotted with maroon; the lips are bright orange. There are no pseudobulbs. Warm-growing.

■ LEFT

PHALAENOPSIS PAIFANG'S GOLDEN LION

Epiphytic orchid. Throughout the year, it produces white flowers that are heavily spotted with rich violet-pink; the lips are rich pink with yellow centres. There are no pseudobulbs. Warm-growing.

■ RIGHT

PHALAENOPSIS SHALU SPOTS
× CARMELA'S PIXIE

Epiphytic orchid. Intermittently
throughout the year, it produces pinkish
red flowers with white centres; the lips
shade to yellow inside and are spotted
darker red. Warm-growing.

■ FAR RIGHT

PHRAGMIPEDIUM ERIC YOUNG

Terrestrial orchid. From summer to
autumn, stems carry a succession of
orange-yellow flowers. Intermediate-
growing.

■ RIGHT

PHRAGMIPEDIUM
LONGIFOLIUM

Terrestrial orchid from Costa Rica,
Panama, Colombia and Ecuador. In
autumn, it produces racemes of light
yellowish green flowers with twisted petal
edges margined with purple, and sepals
veined dark green. The lips are flushed
purple. Cool-growing.

PHRAGMIPEDIUM SCHLIMMII 'WILCOX'

Terrestrial orchid, a selection of a species from Colombia. In summer, it produces a succession of white flowers, flushed pink and shading to yellowish green at the centre, with darker lips ("slippers"). Intermediate-growing.

■ RIGHT

SANDERARA RIPPON TOR 'BURNHAM'

Epiphytic orchid. In summer, it produces flowers that can vary from white to yellow and have red or pink patterning. Cool-growing.

■ RIGHT
SOPHROLAELIOCATTLEYA JEWELER'S ART × C. LODDIGESII

Epiphytic orchid. In spring or autumn (and sometimes at other times of the year), it produces rich purple flowers with lips that are marked deeper purple at the edges and have yellow centres. The pseudobulbs are spindle-shaped. Intermediate-growing.

■ BELOW
SOPHROLAELIOCATTLEYA MARION FITCH 'LA TUILERIE'

Epiphytic orchid. At any time of year, when the pseudobulb is mature, it produces solitary, glowing, pinkish red flowers; the lips are ruffled at the edge. The pseudobulbs are spindle-shaped. Intermediate-growing.

■ BELOW
STANHOPEA TIGRINA

Epiphytic orchid from Mexico. From late summer to autumn, downward-growing stems carry substantial waxy, yellow flowers splashed with deep red. They last for only about three days. The pseudobulbs are cone-shaped and ribbed. Cool- to intermediate-growing. *Stanhopea tigrina* must be grown in a wire or slatted basket that allows the flower stems to push downwards; it sometimes experiences a slow-down in growth in early summer before flowering.

■ LEFT
VUYLSTEKEARA
CAMBRIA 'PLUSH'

Epiphytic orchid. When the pseudobulbs are mature, at varying times of the year, they produce long sprays of vivid crimson flowers with large red and white lips. The pseudobulbs are roughly oval. Cool-growing. *Vuylstekeara* Cambria 'Plush' is one of the most popular orchids of its type and makes an ideal beginner's orchid.

■ RIGHT
VUYLSTEKEARA
LINDA ISLER

Epiphytic orchid. Tall, sometimes branching spikes of rust-red flowers, with lips that have contrasting white borders, emerge when the pseudobulbs are mature. The pseudobulbs are roughly oval. Cool-growing.

■ RIGHT
WILSONARA BONNE NUIT

Large epiphytic orchid. When the
pseudobulbs are mature, they produce tall,
branching spikes carrying masses of showy
yellow flowers that are spotted with brown
and have white lips. The pseudobulbs are
conical and flattened. Cool-growing.

■ LEFT
WILSONARA WIDECOMBE FAIR
'BURNHAM'

Epiphytic orchid. When the pseudobulbs
are mature, they produce long spikes of
white and pink flowers. The pseudobulbs
are conical and flattened. Cool-growing.
Wilsonara Widecombe Fair 'Burnham'
tolerates fluctuating temperatures.

Buying orchids

■ RIGHT
A specialist nursery will have a wide range of plants in flower for sale.

It is best to buy orchids from a specialist nursery. Not only will they have the widest range, but they will also offer advice on which are the most suitable for the conditions you have at home. The orchids will be sold in containers or mounted on bark, as appropriate, and all the materials necessary for their aftercare will also be on sale.

Alternatively, visit an orchid show that will be attended by the major growers. Most exhibitors who attend shows will be able to offer only a fraction of their stock, however, so you may not find exactly the plant you want. Increasingly, orchids are available at larger garden centres, but most offer only a limited range.

Orchids are still relatively expensive plants, since the overheads involved in growing them are higher than for garden plants. They must be raised under glass and grown on until they reach saleable size. Scientific advances in propagation techniques, however, mean that prices are not prohibitively high. Paphiopedilums tend to be expensive, since they do not set seed as freely as other orchids and meristem culture is less successful.

The price usually depends on the size of the plant, with mature plants

of flowering size being the most expensive. Smaller specimens of named varieties are cheaper, but you will need to grow them on for a year or two before they flower. Cheapest of all are unflowered seedlings. In this case, the flower colour (and size)

■ ABOVE
Orchid seedlings are inexpensive, but need to be grown on for a season or two before they will flower.

■ LEFT
Orchids may be sold mounted on bark, if appropriate.

cannot be guaranteed, but the parentage will be known, so you will have a rough idea of what to expect.

If you are a beginner, it is best to restrict your choice to hybrids that have been bred for ease of care. More experienced growers will be tempted by the many attractive species that are available commercially, but these orchids often have much more exacting requirements.

Most commercial growers supply by mail order. If you choose to buy your orchids in this way, it is worth finding out what discounts may be available for bulk orders. Many growers sell collections of plants (for instance cattleyas or cymbidiums) at attractive prices, making these a more economical proposition than buying individual plants; you could spread the costs by clubbing together with other orchid enthusiasts.

Orchids can also be exported. Within the EC, no import permit is required, but this may be necessary for export to countries outside the EC. Nowadays, the orchid trade is international, but you should be aware of any restrictions that exist between countries.

It is illegal to remove orchids from the wild. You should also be wary of the temptation to buy orchids on trips to Singapore, Hong Kong or Thailand, even though they may be considerably cheaper than plants raised locally. They are unlikely to survive the journey home, and besides, have been bred to thrive in the local climate and so may well perish in your home.

How to grow orchids

In order to grow orchids successfully, you need to create an environment that imitates their native habitats. A few terrestrial orchids are suitable for growing outdoors, usually in light, leafy soil in a sheltered site in partial shade, but most need to be grown indoors. Many modern hybrids have been bred specifically to tolerate the conditions found in most houses.

Temperature

For cultivation purposes, orchids can be divided into three broad groups, depending on the typical climate from which the parent species originally came.

Cool-growing orchids originate from high altitudes where nights are

■ LEFT
A maximum–minimum thermometer will record extremes of temperature and help you to maintain the appropriate levels for your plants.

cool, often dropping to 10ºC (50ºF). They need a minimum temperature range of 10–13ºC (50–55ºF) and a maximum of 21–24ºC (70–75ºF).

Intermediate-growing orchids from slightly warmer areas need a minimum temperature of 14–19ºC (57–66ºF) with a maximum of 30–33ºC (86–91ºF).

Warm-growing orchids originating from steamy rainforests have a minimum requirement of 20–24ºC (68–75ºF) and a maximum of 30–33ºC (86–91ºF).

The minimum temperatures are the lowest the plants will tolerate at night in winter. In summer, night-time temperatures can be higher. During the winter, daytime temperatures should be around 3–4ºC (10ºF) higher than at night.

Cymbidiums need fluctuating temperatures between day and night and between summer and winter to stimulate flowering. In winter, the temperature should be allowed to drop to 10ºC (50ºF) at night. During the frost-free months, it is a good idea to place plants outdoors at night,

■ ABOVE
Some plastic containers are designed to hang and have open sides that allow the roots to grow through.

where practical, to ensure the appropriate drop in temperature.

To monitor the temperature, use a maximum–minimum thermometer. Very sophisticated heating systems for use in greenhouses and conservatories are thermostatically controlled and will ensure that the appropriate temperatures are maintained for your plants. In a greenhouse, open the ventilators in summer and leave them open at night.

Light

Most orchids from the tropics are adapted to light levels that remain more or less constant throughout the year. In temperate zones, day length

■ ABOVE
Many orchids (here *Dendrobium* Thai Beauty) are suitable for growing in conventional plastic pots.

■ ABOVE
Vanda rothschildiana in a special plastic basket that does not restrict the growth of the roots.

■ ABOVE
Slatted wooden baskets are suitable for many epiphytes, providing good air circulation around the roots.

fluctuates widely between summer and winter, so the available light needs to be closely monitored. Under glass, orchids need shading in summer to protect them from hot sun and to prevent scorch. In such situations, temperatures can rise much higher than they would in their native habitat. In winter, they need maximum light, and the shading should be removed.

In the home, many orchids will thrive on an east- or west-facing windowsill during the growing season. Screen them from direct light with a muslin blind or net curtain. When dormant in winter, they should be moved to a sill with moderate light. Paphiopedilums,

phalaenopsis and cattleyas (including the intergeneric hybrids with *Sophronitis* and *Laelia*) are ideal candidates for windowsill culture.

Containers

Most orchids can be grown in pots, preferably plastic to allow free drainage of water. Terracotta pots can also be used but tend to retain moisture.

Phragmipediums should be grown in containers that restrict the roots. Epiphytes can also be grown in hanging baskets, and this is a particularly effective way of displaying plants such as stanhopeas or gongoras, which produce trailing

flower stems. You can use either conventional wire baskets or plastic or wooden baskets which are specially made for orchids.

Growing on bark

Some epiphytes are best grown tied to pieces of cork bark or tree-fern fibre, usually with some coconut fibre wrapped around their roots in order to retain moisture. The bark can either be fixed to a wall or hung horizontally to make a "raft". This is an especially effective method of displaying orchids with horizontally spreading rhizomes and hanging flowers such as *Coelogyne massangeana* or *Cytorchis arcuata*.

POTTING MEDIUMS FOR ORCHIDS

Polystyrene (styrofoam) chips used for drainage

Coarsely shredded bark

Bark and coconut fibre

Rockwool, a potting medium favoured by some experienced growers

A coarse compost mix (growing medium) suitable for cattleyas and related genera

A fine but open mix suitable for terrestrials

Composts and other growing mediums

Orchids need special growing mediums that allow swift drainage. Conventional potting composts (potting soils) are unsuitable, being too dense and prone to waterlogging. The best advice is to buy special growing mediums formulated for orchids, which are available from orchid nurseries and larger garden centres; some are specially mixed for particular genera.

Alternatively, you can mix your own growing mediums. For epiphytes, use three parts chopped pine or fir bark to one of coarse grit (or perlite), one of charcoal (to prevent the mixture becoming sour) and one of dry leaves or fibrous peat substitute. A suitable mix for terrestrials is three parts peat substitute, three parts coarse grit, one part perlite and one of charcoal.

Humidity

A humid atmosphere is essential for all orchids. Humidity levels should be kept high during the summer when the plants are in active growth, but can be allowed to fall in winter when they are dormant.

■ RIGHT
Stake tall flower stems (here on a
cymbidium) as they grow.

■ RIGHT
Stake tall flower stems (here on a
cymbidium) as they grow.

■ BELOW
Tall orchids such as *Cymbidium* Maureen
Grapes 'Marilyn' respond well to staking.

In a greenhouse or conservatory,
hose down the floor in the morning
during summer. Repeat in the late
afternoon for warm-growing orchids.
Occasional hosing down may also be
necessary in winter if the heating
system makes the atmosphere dry. Do
not hose down in damp, dull weather.

Mist over the foliage of orchids in
the home twice daily, using rainwater
or softened water to prevent marking
the leaves. Orchids on bark need very
thorough misting, since this is the
only method of providing them with
moisture. During the winter when
they are dormant, they should be
misted occasionally to counteract the
drying effects of central heating.
Paphiopedilums and phalaenopsis
should not be misted, however, as
this can cause rotting of the leaves.

Humidity can also be provided by
standing containers on trays of special
expanded clay pellets available from
orchid nurseries. Growing orchids in
close proximity to each other and to
other plants also increases humidity.

Staking

Orchids with tall flower stems (most
monopodials) need staking, since the
weight of the flowers can cause the

container to fall over. Plunge a thin
stake into the growing medium near
the flower stem as it emerges. As it
grows, tie the shoot to the stake with
short lengths of either wire or twine.
Do not tie it too tightly or you may
cause damage to the stem.

Watering

Water orchids freely while they are in
active growth, using either rainwater
or tapwater, preferably early in the
morning. Make sure that the
containers are well drained and the
plants do not have their feet in water.

In the winter, water less, allowing
the growing medium to dry out
between waterings. Orchids that lose
their leaves in the winter can be kept
dry. Evergreens with pseudobulbs
usually experience a resting phase,
when the water stored in the bulb
will be enough to supply the plant's
needs. Water only to keep the
growing medium barely moist. If the

bulbs begin to look shrivelled, water thoroughly until they plump up again.

Orchids that are more or less permanently in growth, such as cymbidiums, odontoglossums, phalaenopsis and paphiopedilums, which merely experience a slow-down during the cold months, should be watered year round, though less in winter. They should not be allowed to dry out between waterings.

Take care to water directly into the compost (growing medium). If you water from above the plant, water can collect in the leaves, where it can lead to rotting.

Feeding

When orchids are in full growth, feed with a proprietary orchid fertilizer every ten days, or as directed by the manufacturer. Alternatively, use a standard liquid fertilizer for flowering houseplants but at no more than half strength. Orchids should not be fed while dormant. Warm-growing orchids that are kept in growth all year, such as phalaenopsis, can be fed year round, but reduce the frequency of the feed to once every two to three weeks in winter when growth slows down.

Take care not to overfeed; orchids have low nutrient requirements and an excess can be toxic.

Repotting

Orchids usually need potting on when the roots fill the pot. Some orchids will push themselves out of

REPOTTING AN ORCHID

1 This cymbidium has outgrown its container and has started to push itself free with its roots.

2 Slide the orchid from the container and check over the root system. The roots here are healthy and do not need trimming.

3 Select a container the next size up and line the base with polystyrene (styrofoam) chips.

the pot, whilst others relish having their roots restricted and can be left until the roots have emerged from the pot and grip the sides. In most cases, repotting is necessary every other year and is best carried out in spring, just as new growth begins or when the root tips turn green, indicating a renewal in root activity. Alternatively, repot immediately after flowering.

Pot on into containers of the next size up, in order to allow for one or two seasons' growth. Potting on into too large a container will allow

stagnant conditions to develop within the potting medium, which can lead to rotting. In the case of epiphytes, it does not matter if not all the roots will fit into the new container, since they are adapted to exposure to the air, but they can also be trimmed back, if necessary.

Repotting allows you to remove any dead roots from the plant. If you are repotting more than one orchid, disinfect the blade of any knife or scissors you use for this, to prevent the spread of infection from one

plant to another. Repotting also provides a good opportunity for dividing backbulbs.

Use the appropriate growing medium. Orchids need firm potting. Leave a gap of about 2.5cm (1in) between the surface of the growing medium and the rim of the pot in order to allow for watering. Take care not to bury any of the topgrowth. Pseudobulbs should rest on the growing medium surface and not be buried, since this could lead to rotting.

4 Set the plant in position so that the oldest part is in contact with the side of the pot. This leaves plenty of room for the new growth that will occur on the opposite side of the plant. Leave a gap of 2.5cm (1in) at the top of the pot for watering.

5 Feed in fresh compost (growing medium) of the appropriate grade and firm it down with your fingers. (If the orchid is fine-rooted, you may need to use a thin cane for this.)

6 Flood the container with water to settle the plant. Make sure it drains away rapidly so that the roots are not standing in water.

Propagation

Orchids can be propagated by a number of methods, depending on their habit of growth. Propagation is a means of keeping the plants healthy as well as producing new stock. Left to their own devices, they can become quite large specimens, and parts of the plants may become unproductive.

ORCHIDS FROM SEED

Commercial orchid growers regularly raise new hybrids from seed. This practice is also carried out by botanic gardens to raise stocks of endangered species. The dustlike seed is germinated in sterile flasks of nutrient jelly known as Knudson Formula "C", developed in the 1920s. In the case of species, the appropriate root fungus is introduced in order to increase success rates.

Only vegetative methods are suitable for the amateur, but these are relatively easy to carry out and have the added advantage of ensuring that the new plants are identical to the parents. Growing from seed, however, requires laboratory conditions. Commercial growers often practise meristem culture, also in laboratory conditions, which involves growing on tiny scraps of plant tissue in order to produce large stocks of certain plants.

Division

Sympodial orchids such as cattleyas, cymbidiums and odontoglossums can easily be increased by division. The technique is similar to that used for the propagation of herbaceous perennials. Some plants can be easily pulled apart by hand, whilst others will need to be cut apart with a knife or secateurs.

You will need to divide large plants in this way when repotting them. Each division should have at least three active pseudobulbs. Sections of sympodials without pseudobulbs should have two or three growing points.

Old, shrivelled backbulbs should be cut away and discarded, but

PROPAGATION BY DIVISION

1 This orchid, *Coelogyne* Mem. W. Micholitz 'Burnham', has started to climb out of its pot and so is now suitable for dividing.

plump, dormant backbulbs can be separated from the parent and potted up individually.

When potting up the division, the oldest part of the plant should be in contact with the side of the container. This will allow the new growth to develop outwards from the youngest part of the plant. It is also important to ensure that the pseudobulbs are on the compost (growing medium) surface and are not buried.

Keep the divisions well watered in a lightly shaded situation until fresh growth appears.

2 Ease the plant from its container and shake off the old compost (growing medium). Cut through the rhizome with secateurs (shears) or a sharp knife.

3 Gently pull the plant apart with your hands.

4 Cut off any plump, healthy, dormant backbulbs for potting up separately. Each division should have at least three active pseudobulbs and show signs of strong new growth (see inset).

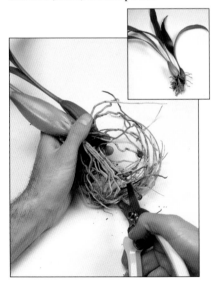

5 Trim back the roots so that the plant will fit easily into its new container (see inset).

6 Position the division in the container so that the oldest bulb is touching the side, allowing maximum room for the new growth.

7 Backfill with the appropriate compost (growing medium) and flood with water to settle the plant well.

PROPAGATION BY BACKBULBS

Adventitious growths

An adventitious growth is one that arises atypically. In the case of monopodial orchids, this refers to plantlets with aerial roots that appear on the nodes (growing points) of the stems. They commonly appear on dendrobiums.

These plantlets (sometimes known as "keikis") can be removed from the parent, provided that they have well-developed roots and leaves. Pot them up in the appropriate growing medium and grow them on in a shady spot. Water them sparingly at

1 Wrap the roots of healthy backbulbs cut from the parent plant (see inset) in moist sphagnum moss.

2 Pot up individually in small pots, firm the moss well, and place in a heated propagator.

first, until the roots are adapted to the compost (growing medium), but mist them frequently.

Keeping the keikis in a heated propagator will accelerate growth but it is not essential.

PROPAGATION FROM KEIKIS

1 This dendrobium has produced several adventitious growths ("keikis").

2 Sever each keiki from the parent with secateurs (shears) or a sharp knife, making sure it has a good root system (see inset).

3 Pot up the keikis individually using fine bark or sphagnum moss.

4 Firm each keiki in well, then water. Place in a heated propagator until signs of strong growth appear.

Stem cuttings

Monopodial orchids can also be increased by stem sections, particularly those that produce long "canes", such as dendrobiums and epidendrums. Cut leafless stems from the parent plant at the start of the growing season and divide them into shorter lengths, each with at least two nodes. Lay these horizontally on trays of moist sphagnum moss and keep them in a humid place out of direct sunlight. New growth should arise after several weeks, when the new plantlets can be potted up in the appropriate compost (growing medium).

PROPAGATION BY STEM CUTTINGS

1 Cut lengths of stem at least 25cm (10in) long from the parent (here *Dendrobium nobile*), cutting just above a node (growing point).

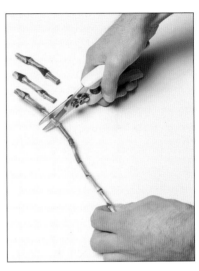

2 Cut each stem into sections, each with at least two nodes.

3 Lay the cuttings on trays of moist sphagnum moss.

4 Place each tray in a clear plastic bag or heated propagator.

5 New growth should appear within three to four months, when the cuttings can be potted up individually. (The moss also grows.)

Pests and diseases

Compared to other indoor plants, orchids suffer from few problems, although those described below can sometimes occur. Proprietary insecticides are available at garden centres, and many list the specific pests they control. Some of the most troublesome insect pests have developed a resistance to pesticides; in such cases, biological controls are more likely to be effective as well as being more environmentally sound. When using any insecticide or fungicide, follow the manufacturer's instructions as to dosage (incorrect doses can be toxic to plants) and safe handling of the product.

Practise good hygiene in the greenhouse by sweeping up dead leaves and other plant material from the floor. If you store empty containers in your greenhouse, check them over regularly and dispose of any slugs and snails that may be sheltering there.

Fungal diseases are often the result of incorrect cultivation. If a plant dies, it may be that it was unsuited to the growing conditions provided, so choose another orchid to replace it.

Bud drop

How to identify: Flower stems develop normally until the buds are on the point of opening. At this stage, they turn yellow and drop off. Phalaenopsis are particularly prone.
Cause: Fumes from heating systems, draughts, lack of sufficient light, over- or under-watering, or too low a temperature can cause it.
Prevention: Maintain good cultivation practices appropriate to the genus. In the case of phalaenopsis, cutting back the flower spike to a fresh node will produce a new flower stem

Petal blight

How to identify: The flowers are blotched and marked with black; white cattleyas are highly susceptible.
Cause: Bright sunlight or faults in cultivation, such as polluted air, cold, wet, or lack of fresh air.
Prevention: When in flower, reduce watering and keep the plants well shaded at an even temperature.

Mealy bugs and scale insects

How to identify: Both are sap-sucking insects that puncture the surface of the leaves. They are clearly visible to the naked eye. Mealy bugs are covered with a white, waxy substance and attack dendrobiums in particular; scale insects have a hard shell that is resistant to chemical sprays. Both can be introduced on new stock.
Control: Use a systemic insecticide.
Prevention: Check any new plants carefully for signs of infestation, and give them any treatment necessary before placing them near other orchids.

Red spider mite

How to identify: The insects themselves are tiny, so you are likely to detect their presence only by the damage they cause: fine stippling of the leaves. In severe cases, the leaves turn yellow and you may find the insects' webs on the undersides. Soft-

leaved lycastes, calanthes and catasetums are particularly vulnerable. The pest thrives in hot, dry conditions.
Control: The most effective method is to introduce the predatory mite *Phytoseiulus persimilis*, available by mail order.
Prevention: Maintain the correct humidity and temperature levels.

False spider mite

How to identify: Pitting appears on the upper sides of leaves. Phalaenopsis are particularly vulnerable. Untreated, fungal infections can take hold, leading to the defoliation of the plant.
Control: As for red spider mite.
Prevention: As for red spider mite.

Caterpillars

How to identify: Leaves and flowers are eaten. Caterpillars will enter greenhouses and conservatories in the summer when doors and windows are left open.
Control: Check over the plants regularly. Pick off the pests by hand and dispose of them.
Prevention: Not usually possible by eco-friendly methods, but maintaining a humid atmosphere will discourage the pests.

Cymbidium mosaic virus

How to identify: Dark, sunken patches appear on the leaves, sometimes in a diamond-shaped pattern. All orchids are susceptible, not just cymbidiums.
Control: None possible; affected plants should be burnt.
Prevention: Control insect pests: the damage they cause to plants allows viruses to take a hold. Practise good hygiene when propagating, and sterilize cutting tools after working on each plant. Isolate any plant that you think may be suffering from virus.

Aphids

How to identify: Flower buds and stems are attacked; flowers – if they open at all – are mottled and distorted. The commonest culprit is the orchid aphid *Cerataphis lataniae*.

■ ABOVE
Cymbidium mosaic virus

Control: Spray with an insecticide or introduce the fly larva predator *Aphidoletes aphidimyza*.
Prevention: Difficult, since aphids are generally endemic, their numbers being dependent on the presence of their natural predators.

Brown spot

How to identify: Soft, watery patches that then turn brown appear on leaves. The disease is caused by the bacterium *Pseudomonas cattleyae*. Phalaenopsis and paphiopedilums are particularly vulnerable.
Control: Cut off all affected areas with a clean, sharp knife. Dust the cut surfaces with a fungicide.
Prevention: Spray susceptible plants periodically with a liquid fungicide.

Slugs and snails

How to identify: Soft leaves are eaten; the pests leave silvery trails. The humid atmosphere in greenhouses attracts slugs and snails.
Control: Water with liquid metaldehyde or use slug pellets.
Prevention: Practise good hygiene by clearing away from the greenhouse floor all plant debris that could provide shelter for the pests.

Orchid checklist

The following checklist provides an at-a-glance reference to the orchids described in this book, as well as to certain others.

Genus	Types of orchid	Cultivation and care
Ada	cool-growing epiphytes	in containers that restrict the roots
Aerangis	intermediate- to warm-growing epiphytes	on an orchid raft or cork slab; flowers hang downwards
Aliceara (*Brassia × Miltonia × Oncidium*)	cool-growing epiphytes	in containers that restrict the roots
Angraecum	warm-growing epiphytes	in baskets
Anguloa	cool- to intermediate-growing epiphytes or terrestrials	in epiphytic or terrestrial compost (growing medium); leaves die back in winter
Bletilla	half-hardy terrestrials	in loam-based compost (soil mix) in containers
Brassavola	cool- to intermediate-growing epiphytes	in slatted baskets or on bark
Brassocattleya (*Brassavola × Cattleya*)	cool- to intermediate-growing epiphytes	in containers
Brassolaeliocattleya (*Brassavola × Cattleya × Laelia*)	cool- to intermediate-growing epiphytes	in containers
Bulbophyllum	cool- to intermediate-growing epiphytes	in slatted baskets or on bark
Calanthe	cool- and warm-growing terrestrials	in containers
Calypso	cool-growing terrestrial (one species only)	in containers; dies back in winter
Cattleya	cool- to intermediate-growing epiphytes	in containers
Coelogyne	cool- to intermediate-growing epiphytes	in containers or hanging baskets
Cymbidium	cool-growing epiphytes and terrestrials	in containers
Cypripedium	hardy to half-hardy terrestrials	in containers in a cool greenhouse; dies back in winter
Dendrobium	cool-growing epiphytes (most) and terrestrials	on bark or in slatted baskets or containers; flower stems need support
Disa	cool-growing terrestrials	in containers; some die back in winter
Doritaenopsis (*Doritis × Phalaenopsis*)	warm-growing epiphytes	in slatted baskets or on bark
Encyclia	cool-growing epiphytes	in slatted baskets; best kept dry in winter
Epidendrum	cool- to intermediate-growing epiphytes and terrestrials	in containers; stems may need support; keep species with pseudobulbs dry in winter
Huntleya	intermediate-growing epiphytes	in containers or on bark
Laelia	cool-growing epiphytes	in containers (large species) or on bark (small ones)
Laeliocattleya (*Laelia × Cattleya*)	cool-growing epiphytes	in slatted baskets
Lemboglossum	cool- to intermediate-growing epiphytes	in containers that restrict the roots
Lycaste	cool-growing epiphytes (most) or terrestrials	in containers; epiphytes also on bark
Masdevallia	cool-growing epiphytes	in containers

Genus	Types of orchid	Cultivation and care
Maxillaria	cool- to intermediate-growing epiphytes (some also terrestrial)	in containers or on bark; keep moist throughout the year
Miltonia	intermediate-growing epiphytes	in containers or slatted baskets or on bark
Miltoniopsis	cool-growing epiphytes	in containers
Odontioda (*Odontoglossum × Cochlioda*)	cool-growing epiphytes	in containers
Odontocidium (*Odontoglossum × Oncidium*)	cool-growing epiphytes	in containers
Odontoglossum	cool-growing epiphytes	in containers
Oncidium	cool- to intermediate-growing epiphytes (most) and terrestrials	in containers (small species) or in baskets or bark (large species); water species without pseudobulbs (or with very small ones) year round
Orchis	hardy terrestrials	in containers in a cool greenhouse or alpine house; outdoors in sheltered areas; dies back in winter
Paphiopedilum	cool- to intermediate-growing terrestrials (most) and epiphytes	in containers that restrict the roots; do not mist
Phaius	intermediate-growing terrestrials	in deep containers
Phalaenopsis	warm-growing epiphytes	in slatted baskets or on bark; flower stems may need support
Phragmipedium	cool-growing epiphytes	in containers in a cool greenhouse or alpine house; dies back in winter
Pleione	terrestrials and epiphytes	in containers in a cool greenhouse or alpine house; dies back in winter
Potinara (*Brassavola × Cattleya × Laelia × Sophronitis*)	cool-growing epiphytes	in containers
Psychopsis	intermediate-growing epiphytes	in containers or on bark
Sophrolaeliocattleya (*Sophronitis × Laelia × Cattleya*)	intermediate-growing terrestrials	in containers
Sophronitis	cool-growing epiphytes	in containers or in slatted baskets or on bark
Spiranthes	cool-growing terrestrials (most) and epiphytes	in containers
Stanhopea	cool- to intermediate-growing epiphytes	in slatted baskets or on bark; flower stems are trailing
Vanda	intermediate-growing epiphytes	in slatted baskets
Vuylstekeara (*Cochlioda × Miltonia × Odontoglossum*)	cool-growing epiphytes	in containers; tolerates warmer conditions
Wilsonara (*Cochlioda × Odontoglossum × Oncidium*)	cool-growing epiphytes	in containers that restrict the roots
Zygopetalum	cool- to intermediate-growing epiphytes or terrestrials	in containers or slatted baskets

Other recommended orchids

In addition to the selection of orchids that are described in the 'Plant catalogue', the following plants are also recommended.

Barkeria skinneri Cool-growing epiphyte from Guatemala with upright sprays of deep lavender-pink flowers highlighted yellow on the lip. Autumn. Needs a winter rest.

***Brassia* Rex** Cool-growing epiphyte which has spiderlike flowers that smell of musk. The sepals and petals are elongated and are sulphur-yellow to lime-green, spotted and marked reddish brown to black; the white lips are also spotted. Summer.

***Brassolaeliocattleya* Holiday Inn** × ***Cattleya* Enid** Cool-growing epiphyte with creamy white flowers that have ruffled petal edges and lips stained rich purple with a yellow centre. Summer–autumn.

***Brassolaeliocattleya* Yellow Imp 'Golden Grail'** Cool- to intermediate-growing epiphyte with bright yellow flowers. Spring or autumn.

Bulbophyllum ornatissimum Cool-growing epiphyte from India with sprays of short-lipped, straw-yellow flowers, dotted and striped purple. Autumn.

Cattleya labiata × **BC Cutty Sark**

Cattleya labiata × ***Brassocattleya* Cutty Sark** Cool- to intermediate-growing epiphyte with white flowers that have ruffled petal edges and lips with yellow centres. Summer–autumn.

Cattleya loddigesii × ***Sophrolaeliocattleya* Jeweler's Art 'Carved Coral'** Cool- to intermediate-growing epiphyte with warm rose-purple flowers that have yellow and darker purple lips. Autumn–spring.

***Cattleya* Silver Flute** × ***Brassolaeliocattleya* Six Bells** Cool- to intermediate-growing epiphyte with pure white flowers that have ruffled petal edges and lips with yellow centres. Summer–autumn.

Cattleya loddigesii × SLC **Jeweler's Art 'Carved Coral'**

Coelogyne cristata Cool-growing epiphyte from the east Himalayas with hanging stems of frosty-white flowers, which are streaked yellow at the throat. Spring. Needs a winter rest.

Coelogyne fimbriata Cool-growing epiphyte from India, and from Vietnam to Hong Kong, with solitary, buff yellow flowers that have white or pale yellow lips marked dark brown. Winter.

Cymbidium erythrostylum Cool-growing epiphyte from Vietnam with brilliant white flowers that have red-striped lips. Spring–summer. Compact.

***Cymbidium* Summer Pearl** Cool-growing epiphyte with upright spikes of creamy white flowers; the lips are heavily spotted with maroon. Summer–spring.

***Doritaenopsis* Alice Girl**

Dendrobium loddigesii Cool-growing epiphyte from south-west China with fragrant, rose-pink flowers that have lips lined and fringed yellow. Early summer. Miniature.

Dendrobium nobile Cool-growing epiphyte from the Himalayas, south China and Taiwan with large, pale pink flowers that have maroon lips. Spring. Needs a winter rest.

Dendrobium senile Cool-growing epiphyte from Burma with golden yellow flowers that have lips fringed with white hairs. Summer.

Dendrobium thyrsiflorum Cool-growing epiphyte from Nepal and Assam with hanging racemes of white or cream flowers that have golden yellow, fringed lips. Summer.

Encyclia
'Sunburst'

Encyclia
brassavolae

Encyclia
radiata

Doritaenopsis **Alice Girl**
Warm-growing epiphyte with erect, branching spikes of pinkish lilac flowers. All year.
Encyclia brassavolae Cool-growing epiphyte from south Mexico to west Panama with racemes of yellowish green to brown flowers that have purple-tipped white lips. Summer–autumn.
Encyclia lancifolia Cool-growing epiphyte from Mexico with spikes of cream or greenish white to yellowish white flowers, streaked with purple, that have green or yellowish green lips. Summer–autumn.
Encyclia radiata Cool-growing epiphyte from Costa Rica, Guatemala, Honduras and Mexico with racemes of scented cream or greenish cream flowers that have lips lined with violet. Summer.

Encyclia 'Sunburst' Cool-growing epiphyte with racemes of light greenish yellow flowers with cream lips. Late summer.
Eria coronaria Cool-growing terrestrial or epiphyte from India that has fragrant cream flowers with pink-marked lips. Spring.
Gomesa crispa Cool-growing epiphyte from Brazil that has dense sprays of scented pale yellowish green flowers. Flowers appear intermittently throughout the year.
Laelia anceps Cool-growing epiphyte from central Mexico with tall stems of soft lilac flowers that have deep mauve lips with yellow centres. Autumn–winter. Requires a period of rest during the winter.

Laelia **Seagull** Cool-growing epiphyte with sprays of small flowers in shades of orange. Summer.
Laeliocattleya **Callistoglossa** Cool- to intermediate-growing epiphyte with very large, pure white flowers that have ruffled petal edges and lips stained yellow at the centre. Summer–autumn.
Laeliocattleya **Canhamiana 'Coerulea'** Cool-growing epiphyte with large, showy, blue flowers that have darker lips. Winter–spring.
Laeliocattleya **Gila Wilderness 'Majestic'** Cool-growing epiphyte with large, reddish purple flowers that have flared petals. Summer.
Laeliocattleya **Lake Cachuma** Cool-growing epiphyte with large, showy, lavender flowers. Autumn or spring.

Laeliocattleya **Lilac Dream** × **Casitas Spring** Cool-growing epiphyte with sumptuous, solitary, pink-flushed white flowers that have lips with yellow centres and pinkish violet edges. Summer.
Laeliocattleya **Magic Bell 'New Trick'** Cool-growing epiphyte with white flowers, marked yellow and orange, that have trumpet-shaped yellow and orange lips. Winter–spring. Compact.
Laeliocattleya **Peak Season** Cool-growing epiphyte with large, showy, lavender purple flowers that have yellow and darker purple lips. Autumn–spring.
Laeliocattleya **Rojo 'Mont Millais'** Cool-growing epiphyte which has racemes of cinnabar-red flowers. Winter.

**Laeliocattleya Lilac Dream ×
Casitas Spring**

**Odontocidium
Purbeck Gold**

**Oncidium
macranthum**

Masdevallia **Urubamba**
Cool-growing epiphyte with
short stems that carry solitary
flowers with brilliant red
sepals, spotted darker,
surrounding insignificant
petals and lip. It lacks
pseudobulbs. Summer.
Do not allow to dry out
in winter.

Masdevallia veitchiana ×
schmidt-mummii Cool-
growing epiphyte with
solitary flowers that have
brilliant red, long-tailed sepals
surrounding insignificant
petals and lips. It lacks
pseudobulbs. Summer.
Do not allow to dry out
in winter.

Maxillaria picta Cool-
growing epiphyte from
Colombia and Brazil with
fragrant, yellow flowers,
spotted red outside. Winter.

Maxillaria tenuifolia Cool-
growing epiphyte from
Mexico to Honduras and
Nicaragua with coconut-
scented, deep red, yellow-
lipped flowers. Summer.

Miltoniopsis **Anjou 'St
Patrick'** Cool-growing
epiphyte with deep crimson
flowers that have lips flared
with brilliant orange and
white at the centre. Mainly
summer, occasionally at other
times of the year.

Miltoniopsis **Bremen × Lilac
Surprise** Cool-growing
epiphyte with white flowers
marked deep maroon. Mainly
summer, occasionally at other
times of the year.

Miltoniopsis **Hamburg**
Cool-growing epiphyte with
deep red flowers with yellow
on the lips. Mainly summer,
occasionally at other times.

Miltoniopsis **St Helier**
Cool-growing epiphyte with
pink flowers edged white
and with maroon "masks".
Mainly summer, occasionally
at other times.

Odontioda **Honiton
Lace 'Burnham'** Cool-
growing epiphyte with tall
sprays of large, mauve and
pink flowers. Flowering
season varies.

Odontioda **Rialto ×
Odontocidium** **Panse** Cool-
growing epiphyte with sprays
of creamy white flowers,
blotched with yellow, that
have frilled petal edges.
Flowering season varies.
Neat-growing.

Odontobrassia **Aztec** Cool-
growing epiphyte with long-
lasting sprays of large, showy,
starlike, rust-red flowers.
Flowering season varies.

Odontocidium **Hansueli
Isler** Cool-growing epiphyte
with tall, branching spikes of
large, bright yellow and
brown flowers. Flowering
season varies.

Odontocidium **Purbeck
Gold** Cool-growing epiphyte
with rich yellow flowers
mottled with brown.
Mainly autumn, occasionally
at other times.

Odontoglossum cordatum ×
Oncidium ghiesbrechtianum
Cool-growing epiphyte with
flowers in various shades of
brown that have yellow to
copper-red lips. Flowering
season varies.

Odontoglossum **Royal
Occasion** Cool-growing
epiphyte with white
flowers and lips that are
marked with golden yellow.
Early summer.

Phalaenopsis aramanthes ×
Orglades Tartan

Phalaenopsis
Brother Goldstone

Sophrolaeliocattleya Rocket
Burst 'Deep Enamel'

Oncidium longipes Cool- to
intermediate-growing
epiphyte from south-east
Brazil with short racemes of
yellow flowers, spotted and
streaked reddish brown, that
have solid yellow lips. Spring–
summer. Small.
Oncidium macranthum
(syn. *Cyrtolichum*
macranthum) Cool- to
intermediate-growing
epiphyte from Colombia,
Ecuador and Peru with tall,
spreading panicles of golden
yellow flowers that have lips
edged purple. Summer.
Paphiopedilum **Chiquita**
Cool- to intermediate-
growing terrestrial with soft
yellow flowers. Spring–
summer.
Paphiopedilum **Crossianum**
Cool- to intermediate-
growing terrestial with
pinkish flowers. Winter.

Paphiopedilum insigne
Cool- to intermediate-
growing terrestrial from
north-east India and eastern
Nepal with slipper-shaped,
copper-brown flowers that
have yellow dorsal petals.
Autumn–spring.
Paphiopedilum **Leeanum**
Cool- to intermediate-
growing terrestrial with small
green flowers, which are
spotted darker, and coppery
"pouches". Winter.
Paphiopedilum **Stone**
Ground Intermediate-
growing terrestrial with a
succession of large flowers
that have purple "pouches"
and drooping petals. Winter.
Phalaenopsis aramanthes ×
Orglades Tartan Warm-
growing epiphyte with pale
pink flowers veined darker
that have soft rose-pink lips.
Any time of year.

Phalaenopsis **Brother**
Goldstone Warm-growing
epiphyte with cream flowers
that are heavily mottled with
rich reddish pink. The lips
are marked with brilliant
orange-red and yellow. Any
time of year.
Phalaenopsis **Follett** Warm-
growing epiphyte with white
to pale pink flowers striped
deeper pink. Any time of year.
Pleione formosana Cool-
growing terrestrial from east
China and Taiwan with soft
lilac flowers that have white
lips marked brown and
purplish pink. Spring. Dies
back in winter.
Sophrolaeliocattleya
Jewel Box 'Dark Waters'
Cool- to intermediate-
growing epiphyte with rich
deep red flowers that have
trumpet-shaped lips.
Autumn–spring.

Sophrolaeliocattleya
Rocket Burst 'Deep Enamel'
Intermediate-growing
epiphyte with brilliant
orange-red flowers. Any time
of year.
Vanda **Rothschildiana**
Intermediate-growing
epiphyte with hanging
racemes of violet-blue flowers,
that are veined darker.
Intermittently throughout
the year.
Wilsonara **Kolibri** Cool-
growing epiphyte with tall,
branching spikes of small
but showy, deep pink and
purple flowers. Flowering
season varies.
Zygopetalum **Artur Elle**
Cool- to intermediate-growing
epiphyte with tall spikes of
large, fragrant flowers that are
patterned green and brown
and have lips veined purple.
Autumn–spring.

Index

Page numbers in *italics* refer to illustrations.